This edition published by Parragon Books Ltd in 2017

Parragon Books Ltd
Chartist House
15–17 Trim Street
Bath BA1 1HA, UK
www.parragon.com

ISBN 978-1-4748-7648-3

T#547132

Printed in China

PUPPY BIRTHDAY TO YOU!

Bath · New York · Cologne · Melbourne · Delhi
Hong Kong · Shenzhen · Singapore

One windy afternoon in Adventure Bay, a box moved down the street towards Katie's Pet Parlour. But this box wasn't being blown by the wind. It was creeping down the street on eight paws!

Suddenly, a big gust blew the box away, revealing Skye and Rubble underneath. The pups scampered into the parlour.

Inside, Ryder, Katie and Rocky were getting ready for Chase's surprise birthday party.

"Who's making sure Chase doesn't surprise us while we set up?" Skye asked.

"Marshall," Rocky replied. "He can keep a secret ... can't he?"

Across town, Marshall and Chase were playing in the Pup Park. They swung on the swings and slid down the slide.

"Maybe we should go and find Ryder and the pups," Chase said.

"No!" said Marshall. "We can't! Because it's, um, so nice out here."

Just then, the wind picked up again and blew them right across the park!

Back at the Pet Parlour, the lights suddenly went dark and Katie's electric mixer stopped.

"All the lights on the street are out," Rocky said.

Ryder thought he knew what was wrong. "PAW Patrol, to the Lookout!"

The team raced to the Lookout. But the electric
doors wouldn't open. Luckily, Rocky had a screwdriver,
which did the trick.

Once they were inside, Ryder used his telescope to check Adventure Bay's windmills.

"Just as I thought," he said. "The wind has broken a propeller. Since the windmill can't turn, it can't make electricity. We need to fix it!"

Ryder looked at Rocky. "We'll need something from your truck to fix the broken blade."

"Green means go!" Rocky said, preparing for action.

"We'll need Marshall's ladder to climb up and fix the windmill," said Ryder.

Marshall nodded. "I'm fired up!"

"Chase, the traffic lights won't work without electricity," Ryder continued. "I need you to use your siren and megaphone to direct traffic."

"These paws uphold the laws," Chase said.

Meanwhile, Skye, Zuma and Rubble
raced back to the Pet Parlour to continue
setting up for Chase's surprise party.
It was very dark, but Katie had a torch.

In the centre of town, Chase busily directed traffic.
"You're our hero," Mayor Goodway said as she
crossed the street safely.
"I'm just doing my PAW Patrol duty," Chase said.

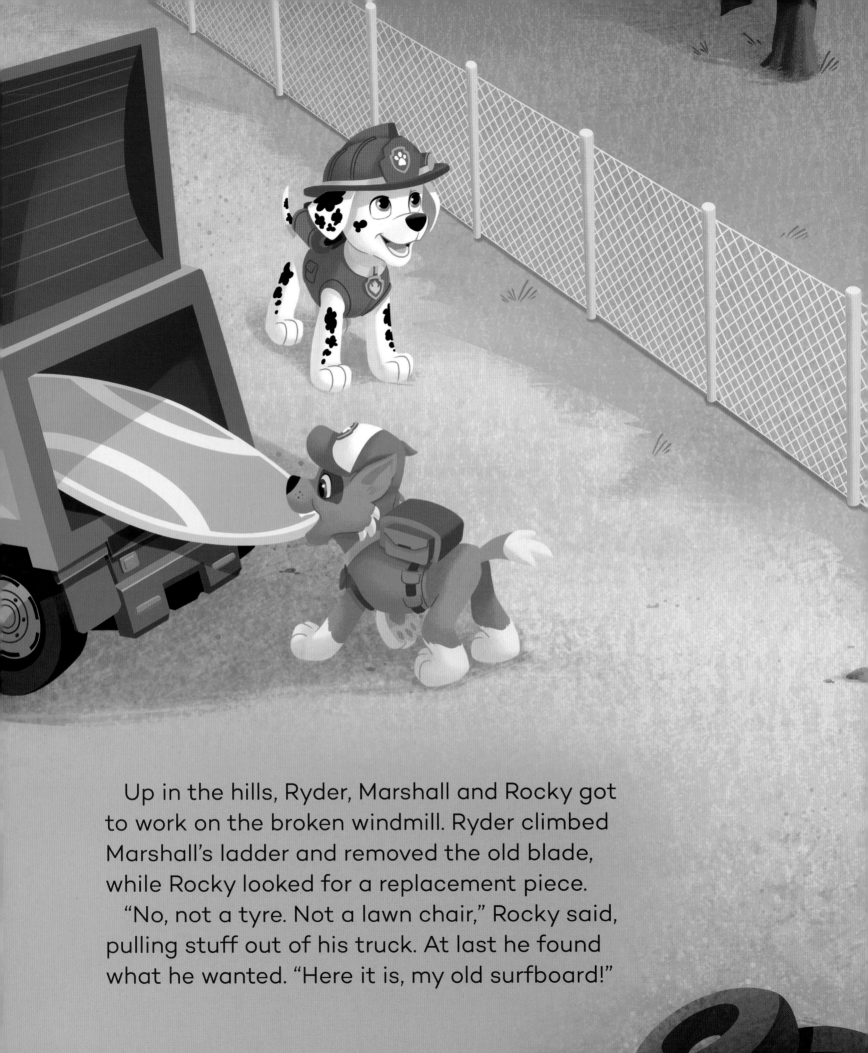

Up in the hills, Ryder, Marshall and Rocky got to work on the broken windmill. Ryder climbed Marshall's ladder and removed the old blade, while Rocky looked for a replacement piece.

"No, not a tyre. Not a lawn chair," Rocky said, pulling stuff out of his truck. At last he found what he wanted. "Here it is, my old surfboard!"

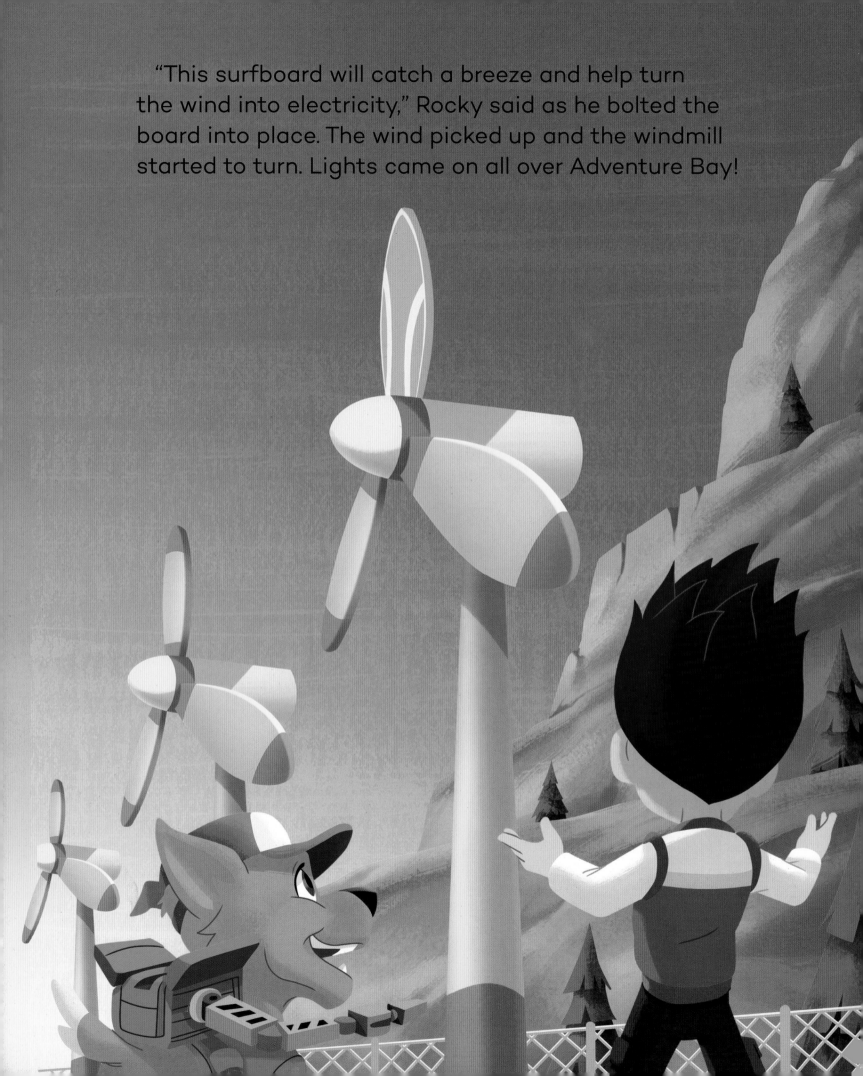

"This surfboard will catch a breeze and help turn the wind into electricity," Rocky said as he bolted the board into place. The wind picked up and the windmill started to turn. Lights came on all over Adventure Bay!

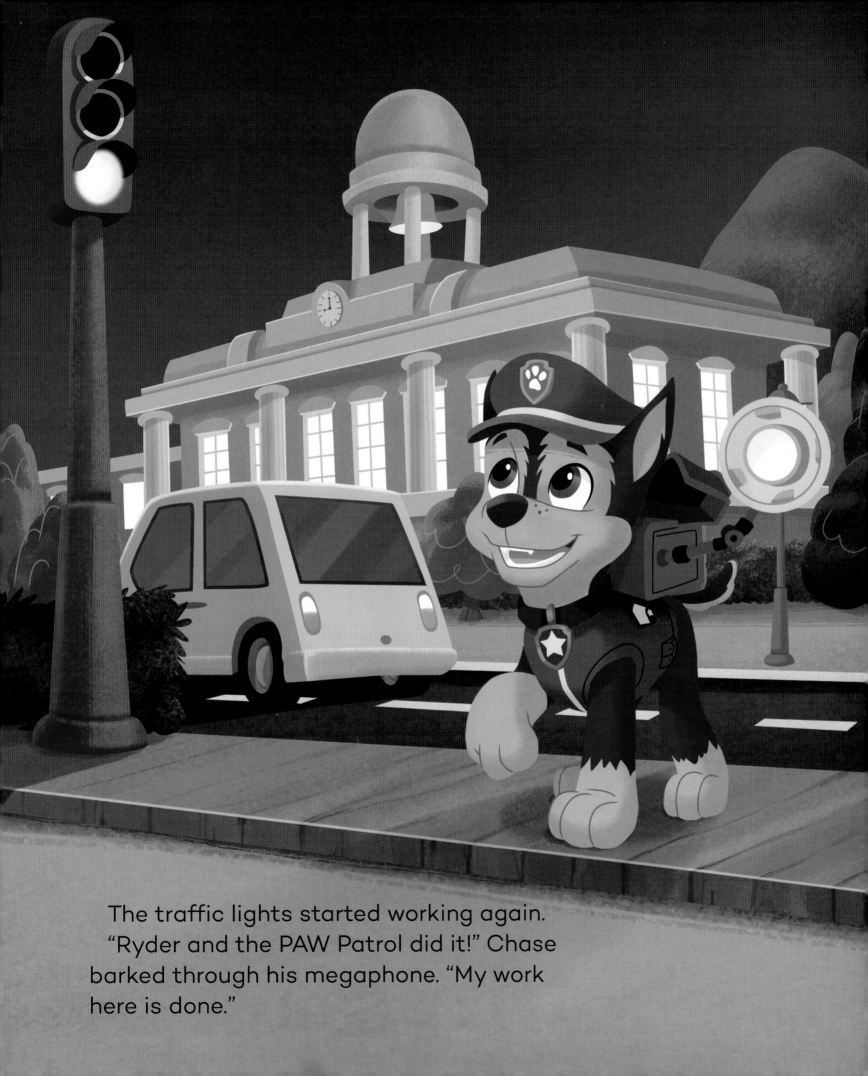

The traffic lights started working again.
"Ryder and the PAW Patrol did it!" Chase
barked through his megaphone. "My work
here is done."

The lights in the Pet Parlour glowed brightly.

"Hooray!" cheered Skye, but then she frowned. "Aw! There's no time to make a cake."

Katie thought for a moment. "I have an idea."

As Chase drove back to the Lookout, he got a call from Ryder. "We need you at Katie's— in a hurry!"

When Chase got there, everything was dark and quiet.

Chase stepped inside. The lights went on. "SURPRISE!" everyone yelled.

Chase was amazed. "Wow! You guys turned the lights back on *and* made a party for me?"

"We didn't have time to bake you a real cake," Katie said, "so we hope you like your pup-treat cookie cake."

"Whenever it's your birthday, just yelp
for help!" Ryder said with a laugh.
All the puppies cheered and enjoyed
a taste of Chase's special cake.

The End